Skate Expectations

McGee & Me! books and videos available
from Word Publishing

Focus on the Family

P R E S E N T S

Skate
Expectations

WORD PUBLISHING

WORD (UK) Ltd
Milton Keynes, England

WORD AUSTRALIA
Kilsyth, Victoria, Australia

STRUIK CHRISTIAN BOOKS (PTY) LTD
Maitland, South Africa

ALBY COMMERCIAL ENTERPRISES PTE LTD
Balmoral Road, Singapore

CHRISTIAN MARKETING NEW ZEALAND LTD
Havelock North, New Zealand

JENSCO LTD
Hong Kong

SALVATION BOOK CENTRE
Malaysia

This one's for my Nick

SKATE EXPECTATIONS

ISBN 0-85009-285-X (Australian ISBN 1-86258-098-7)

Front cover illustration copyright © 1989 by Morgan Weistling
Interior illustrations by Nathan Greene, copyright © 1989 by
Tyndale House Publishers, Inc.

McGEE & ME! is a trade mark of Living Bibles International
copyright © 1989 by Living Bibles International.

Printed and bound in Great Britain for Word (U.K.) Ltd by Cox &
Wyman Ltd., Reading

90 91 92 93 / 10 9 8 7 6 5 4 3 2 1

Contents

Love is very patient and kind, never jealous or envious, never boastful or proud, never haughty or selfish or rude. Love does not demand its own way. It is not irritable or touchy. It does not hold grudges and will hardly even notice when others do it wrong. It is never glad about injustice, but rejoices whenever truth wins out.

If you love someone, you will be loyal to him no matter what the cost. You will always believe in him, always expect the best of him, and always stand your ground in defending him. (1 Corinthians 13:4-7, *The Living Bible*).

ONE
Beginnings . . .

I could feel the surge of electrons pulse through my body as I began to demolecularize (you know, when your body dissoves "Star Trek" style). Then suddenly the time transporter started to backfire. Doggone, good for nothing, cheap time transporter. I knew I should have bought a name brand.

It wheezed, it coughed, it sputtered. Then it began to shake, rattle, and roll. Next it was probably going to play a song from the fifties, or—worse yet—the theme from "Happy Days." I knew I was in real trouble, so I hopped out of the transporter chamber as fast as my cute little tootsies could carry me. (I mean, being demolecularized in a fritzed-out time transporter is about as much fun as sticking your tongue into an electrical outlet. That's something I wouldn't recommend to anyone unless he was a rechargeable battery.)

Time was running out. My arch rival, the sinister Dr. Dastardly, had already time-ported back into the twentieth century. I had to follow him, and quickly. But that's all right; "quickly" is my middle name.

I raced to the control panel to see what was wrong. I didn't see anything unusual—just the tools of your everyday superintellectual genius. An Etch-a-Sketch® toy here, a few Spiderman comic books there, a zillion and a half Reese's Pieces wrappers, and 328 empty Diet Pepsi cans in the corner. We intellectual genius types can get kind of thirsty. (We also tend to have a little weight problem.)

Then I spotted it . . . someone had set a Captain Crunch ice cream bar on top of the control panel just above the Zittron-Ray tube. The heat from the tube had melted the ice cream bar, and the gooey goodness had oozed all over the tube's circuits.

I grabbed the tube and did what any junk-food addict would do. I began to lick—fast. Soon that puppy was cleaner than a kid's candy bag the day after Halloween.

I put the tube back in place and raced to the chamber as the transporter crackled back to life. Any moment I'd be hurled through time. Back to the twentieth century. Back to the good ol' days where you could still buy a Big Mac for under thirty bucks. Back to where Dr. Dastardly was at this very minute trying to change history for his devious purposes.

No one knows when the doctor's mind first snapped—when he decided to use his genius to destroy civilization. Some say it was after opening three Cracker Jack boxes in a row without finding a prize. Others say it happened when his mother made him eat too much cooked cauliflower. Then

10

there is the Twenty-Four-Hours-of-Watching-MTV-without-a-Break theory.

Whatever the reason, he had become a terrible menace. He built a time travel machine (sorta like mine, but without the nice shiny knobs), then kept traveling back into time to try to destroy history—or at least mess it up a lot.

Like the time he went back and almost convinced Paul Revere to catch a flick at the local mall instead of taking his little horsy for a moonlight ride.

Then there was the time Dastardly visited the inventor of Popsicles. That was a close one. I mean, he almost convinced the guy to use pickles instead. (So the next hot summer day when you go in for a Popsicle be sure to thank me. If I hadn't been there to stop the Doc, you'd probably be biting into a nice frozen dill on a stick. Yum, yum.)

No one knew what Dr. Dastardly had in mind this time . . . but whatever it was, he had to be stopped. And there was only one person who could stop him: Me, the incredibly good-looking and ever-so-humble Time Tracker.

Faster than you can say "demolecularized," I found myself back in the twentieth century. As I looked around I saw I was in some sort of small, darkened chamber. Dastardly was there, too. I knew it. I had a nose for that kind of thing. (The fact that I'd slipped half a pound of garlic in his lunch before he left was also a help.)

"Dastardly," I called.

There was no answer. What I did hear was some muffled murmurings outside the chamber. It sounded like some woman was giving directions.

But I had no time to worry about that. I had to find Dastardly before he could do any real damage to history.

I silently moved around the room listening for Dastardly's breath. Well, actually, I was smelling for it. Suddenly a book the size of a Cincinnati Bengals left-tackle tumbled from nowhere and pinned me to the ground. Then another. And another. Until I was buried beneath a two-ton pile of reading material.

Now for normal mortals that might have been the end. But for a Time Tracker, it was just a part of the job. With my near-superhuman strength I pushed the books aside and staggered back to my feet. I heard a loud rumble and spun around to see a load of giant No. 2 pencils rolling toward me. Before I could throw my incredibly agile body into reverse they knocked me to the ground, flatter than a soccer ball that had played tag with a semi.

I tried to focus my eyes, but all I could see were stars—Batman here, Rocky there, Superman, Indy . . . who invited these guys, anyway? I gave my head a shake and they disappeared. That figured. Just when you need a superhero there isn't one to be found. And believe me I could have used one right then because ol' Doc Dastardly was coming right at me! I couldn't see him, but his breath was so strong I could feel my contacts starting to melt.

That mysterious female voice continued in the background as Dastardly and I started to fight. First we staggered to the left, than to the right. Back and forth. Back and forth. It was like some kinda crazy dance. In fact, it was a dance. Before I knew it we were doing the fox-trot, then a waltz.

Then we started putting our left feet in and our left feet out and our left feet in and shaking them all about. I loved the Hokey Pokey, and the Doc was amazingly good (for a notoriously no-good nutcase). But before I could compliment him he suddenly pushed the button on his remote control time travel wristwatch and disappeared.

Rats. I hate it when he does that. He had escaped into another century. And without even finishing the dance. Who knew what mischief he was planning next? Or where.

Still, *I thought as I broke into a boyish grin that only us incredibly handsome crime fighters know how to grin,* let him go where he will. He won't be too hard to follow. Not for me—McGee, the great Time Tracker. Besides, nobody with all that garlic on his breath can hide for long.

I sighed, then pushed open the lid above me and poked my head out of Nick's desk. Oh, in case you're confused, we weren't really fighting in a darkened chamber. Actually, we'd been fighting in Nick's school desk. In fact, the whole Doc Dastardly episode was just another of my mind-boggling imaginary adventures.

I peered over the edge of Nick's desk, out into the school room. A-ha, just as I suspected. That mysterious female voice I'd heard earlier was Mrs. Harmon, Nick's teacher.

I glanced over to the clock to see how much time I had before school was out. Hmm. Less than a minute. Oh well, I could always finish this imaginary game some other day. Right now I'd better hop back inside and start straightening up. All that book throwing and pencil rolling had made quite a mess. And Time Trackers never leave messes.

T minus 45 seconds and counting . . .

Mrs. Harmon stood at the chalkboard finishing her talk on the day's geography lesson. She went on and on and on. And just when you thought she was through, she went on some more.

"So when you want to remember the Great Lakes," she said looking very pleased with what she was about to say. "Simply think of one word." She turned and wrote five letters on the board: "H-O-M-E-S."

Nick stared blankly at the board. He was thinking of homes all right. But not the homes Mrs. Harmon meant. He was thinking about the home where he had good times with McGee and adventures at his drawing table. Most importantly, he was thinking of the home he could get to by using his brand new skateboard.

Ah, yes, the skateboard.

He threw a glance to the clock: *T minus 37 seconds and counting.* If he could just make it through the next thirty-seven seconds without dying . . . if he could just hang on a few more seconds until school was out, he'd be on that skateboard. He'd be flying around those curves. He'd be feeling the wind against his face. He'd be—

"Now who can tell me what the *H* stands for?" Mrs. Harmon's voice was a dull buzz in the background. It reminded Nick of a pesky fly. The type that really doesn't bother you, but that you wouldn't miss if it was gone.

It's not that he disliked Mrs. Harmon. She was a great teacher. After all, she was the one who helped him all those extra hours with his fractions—you know, his numerators and denominators and all that stuff. Stuff he knew would be of use to him someday. But "someday" wasn't his problem. Right now his problem was getting through *this* day.

"Renee, can you tell me what the *H* stands for?"

Renee was one of Nick's friends. She was pretty smart and she was pretty cool—for a girl, that is.

"Uh, Lake Huron?" Renee guessed.

"Exactly," Mrs. Harmon beamed as she wrote the name beside the letter *H*. She was obviously pleased to discover some sign of life in her classroom. "And what about the *O*?"

T minus 22 seconds. . . .

Nicholas had spent a long time saving up for that skateboard. Nearly seven months. Ever since his first board disappeared from the moving van (along with his bike and a few other items. That was one of the disadvantages of moving into the city).

Back home—back in the suburbs where he used to live—he'd gotten pretty good on his skateboard. In fact, he was one of the top skateboarders in his school.

Of course, that was seven months ago. Seven months was a long time. It had seemed even longer when Nick hopped on his board that morning and rode to school. Talk about rusty. I mean, try as he might, some of the old moves just weren't there. It was like his mind knew what to

do but his body had forgotten how to do it.

Nick wasn't worried though. All he needed was a few more weeks of practice.

"Philip, can you tell me what the letter *O* stands for?" Mrs. Harmon's voice cut into Nick's thoughts.

Nick glanced over to Philip. He was a cute kid for a munchkin. I mean, this guy was so short he needed a stepladder just to get into his high tops. It was too bad, though, because people were always picking on him just because he was short. Nicholas could never figure that out. Why would everybody gang up on one kid like that? Nick frowned. You'd never catch *him* doing that. No sir. 'Course you'd never catch him hanging around the kid either. I mean, after all, Nick had a reputation to keep up.

One thing was for sure, though—ol' Philip was one smart kid. What this guy lacked in height he definitely made up for in brains.

"Lake Ontario," the little guy chirped confidently.

"Very good, Philip," Mrs. Harmon said as she wrote 'Ontario' next to the *O*.

Nick took another peek at the clock.

T minus fourteen . . .

He looked back toward Mrs. Harmon. 'Course he never really saw her. That was a gift he developed long ago . . . pretending to pay attention in class while his mind was a million miles away. Right now though, his mind wasn't exactly a million miles away. It was just outside on the sidewalk doing sensational 360s, rails, and some incredible boardwalking.

In the midst of it all, he began counting down: *T*

minus thirteen, twelve, eleven, ten . . .

"Now how about *M*?" Mrs. Harmon said. "Anyone?"

Nick had to grin. This woman just didn't know when to quit.

Nine, eight, seven . . .

"Anyone at all?" By now all eyes were glued to the clock. It was pretty obvious no one was paying any attention and it was pretty obvious Mrs. Harmon was getting a little frustrated.

Then it happened. Nick glanced up, and Mrs Harmon caught his eye! Oh no, how could this be?! Any kid in his right mind knows that if you let the teacher make eye contact you're in for it. If they catch your eye they'll think you're actually paying attention. And if they think you're paying attention they may, in desperation, ask *you* the question. How could he have been so stupid? How could he have let this happen?

Six, five . . .

"Nicholas?"

Four . . .

Nick froze. What was she talking about? Something about the Great Lakes? Some letters? Some name? He swallowed hard and tried to smile.

Three . . .

She kept waiting. The pleasant look on her face was beginning to look a lot less pleasant.

Two . . .

Nick tried to swallow again. But it felt more like he was choking. He was trapped. There was nothing he could do but fake it.

One . . .

He opened his mouth and began to say something. What, he wasn't sure. But he'd have to say something, anything. And then it happened. . . .

Rinngg.

The bell! That wonderful sound. That blessed, beautiful bell. That splendiferous sound that was a symphony to any fifth-grader's ears. Nick was saved. Off the hook. Yes-siree, life was good.

All the kids were up and on their feet. But Mrs. Harmon wasn't finished yet. Sure, kids like Nick had certain tricks to fake out their teachers. But teachers like Mrs. Harmon have a few little tricks of their own.

"Hold it!" she called. "Hold it a minute!" The kids came to a stop. "Since all of you have been working so hard this afternoon,"—there was no missing the sarcasm in her voice—"I've prepared a little take-home geography quiz. You may pick them up as you leave."

The kids let out more than their usual groans as they filed past her desk to pick up the quiz.

"I'll collect them first thing tomorrow." Mrs. Harmon's voice was much more pleasant now. In fact she was practically smiling. "Oh, by the way, your textbooks do *not* have all the answers. So I hope you were paying attention today."

There were more groans from the kids, followed by more smiling from Mrs. Harmon. Chalk one up for her. Teacher: One. Kids: Zilch.

TWO
Easy Words

At last we were free and heading home. Now I
could put all of my great skateboarding knowledge
to use. Now I could begin sharing my years of ex-
perience, my incredible moves, my breathtaking
technique with my number one, adoring fan . . .
Nicholas Martin.

Yes, as unbelievable as it sounds I was once a
star skateboarder. I had even appeared in such
shows as "ABC's Wide World of Dorks," and the
ever-popular "That's Regrettable!"

And why not? After all, I'm the one who invented
the famous Hang Eight Move. (It would have been
Hang Ten, but us cartoon characters only have
eight toes. Hmm, I'll have to talk to Nick about that.)

That was only the beginning of my fame. Soon
skateboard manufacturers from all over the world
were coming to me. I mean, these guys were offer-
ing me money, cars, houses . . . anything to get me
to sign contracts promising that I wouldn't use any
of their equipment in public.

21

Yes-siree-bob, I was definitely a legend in my own mind . . . uh, time . . . whatever. Now it was time to pass on my great pearls of wisdom.

"Hey, Nick! You coming or what?" It was Louis hollering from across the playground.

"Nah," my little buddy called back. "I'm going to board home. See you tomorrow."

Louis gave a nod and headed off toward the buses.

Great, I thought. Now I can crawl out of my sketchpad and ride on Nicholas's shoulders. Not that I mind the sketchpad. I mean, I've really fixed the place up since you saw it last. Got a big-screen TV in the den now, not to mention the hot tub and barbecue out on the patio. But ever since Nick left that liverwurst sandwich in his backpack, which was out all afternoon in the hot sun . . . well, let's just say the neighborhood definitely has an air about it.

As we came around the back of the school Nicholas suddenly stopped.

"Hey, Dude," I called in my best surfer voice. "Like, what's happening?" Then I saw them.

Derrick, undisputed winner of the All-School Bully Award, and a couple of his thugs-in-training had little Philip pushed up against the wall. I mean, talk about having a crush on somebody. They had ol' Philip pressed so flat he couldn't move.

"You want these?" Derrick sneered. He held Phil's backpack high over his head . . . and then dumped out all the papers, books, pencils, and allergy medicine on the ground.

I wanted to get in there and fight. To practice my

22

judo, karate, kung fu . . . and all the other Chinese words I know. (I have a great vocabulary.) But for some reason Nick pulled back around the corner to hide.

This isn't right, I thought. We should be in there doing something. But Nick had this thing about pain and death. I guess he figured he was allergic to them. The last thing in the world he wanted to do was break out in a bad case of bruises and crushed bones.

"Check his pockets," one of Derrick's Dorks ordered.

They did.

"Nah, he don't have no money."

It was getting so bad I had to do something. I mean, I couldn't just stand and watch the little guy get clobbered. I couldn't watch him go through all that pain and misery. I couldn't stand seeing any more anguish and agony. So, finally I did what had to be done . . . I covered my eyes.

After a few more thwacks and oofs, Derrick and his Dorks were through.

Unfortunately, so was little Philip. I opened my eyes just in time to see him slowly slide down the wall to the ground. Immediately Nick and I were at his side.

"Hey, you OK?" Nicholas asked.

"Yeah," Philip squeaked. "I guess."

But if you ask me I'd say he guessed wrong. Nick reached over and started gathering Philip's books and papers before the wind could blow them away. "Why was Derrick picking on you?" he asked.

The little guy looked up at Nick. "Don't tell Mrs.

Harmon, but he's making me do his answers to the geography quiz."

Nicholas let out a loud snort. "Figures," he said. "I guess Derrick can't handle all those big words . . . like 'Ohio.' Listen, if I were you I wouldn't do it."

Atta boy, Nick, I thought. You took the words right out of my ever-so-glib mouth.

"But I gotta," Philip insisted. "If I don't—"

"Why don't you just give him the wrong answers?" Nicholas broke in. "I bet that'd teach him a lesson! And it sure wouldn't be the first time Derrick flunked a quiz." He finished with a little chuckle.

Philip looked at him and smiled, then they both rose to their feet.

"You sure you're all right?" Nick asked. "Got everything?"

"Yeah," the little munchkin croaked. "Thanks."

Nicholas gave a nod and we headed off.

I could feel Philip's eyes on us as we left. Yes-siree-bob, another satisfied customer. I tell you, this fighting for truth, justice, and the American way isn't half bad. We'd done the right thing—the thing we always hear about in Sunday school. We'd chosen to "love" Philip. Gosh, we were great.

The more I thought about it the more I figured this love business was OK. It really wasn't that tough. A few extra minutes. A few easy words. No biggie. I wondered why people made such a big deal out of it. Seemed to me "loving your neighbor" was a piece of cake.

It wouldn't be long before I realized I might have been just a teensy-weensy bit wrong . . .

Later that evening, Nick's older sister Sarah was having her own education in love—real love. Not small-time love, mind you, or boyfriend-girlfriend love or "being-nice-to-a-weird-little-brother" love. This was the kind of love that's drastic—even more drastic than giving up the phone for someone else to use. We're talking *major* love and sacrifice. We're talking . . . babysitting on a Saturday afternoon!

"But Mom . . . "

"If they don't find a babysitter," Mom said as she reached for the plates in the cupboard, "they'll spend all their time taking care of little Carol instead of enjoying the wedding." She handed the plates to Sarah.

Sarah let out a sigh of frustration as she began to set the table for dinner. "They" were the Robinsons from down the street. The wedding was their niece's. "Little Carol" was the Robinson's spoiled little daughter, who was also the rottenest kid in the whole neighborhood. Better make that the city. (In fact, if they were to have a Miss USA Spoiled Brat Contest, guess who'd be holding the roses and wearing the crown!)

Sarah had babysat Carol once before. And once was enough. Maybe it had something to do with the way the little girl smeared raspberry jam all over the fridge. "Mommy always lets me finger paint," she insisted. Or maybe it was the way she took the scissors and snipped down all of Mommy's prized Boston ferns. Or maybe it was when she tried to flush Kitty down the toilet. In any case, Sarah knew the kid meant trouble.

But there was another reason Sarah didn't want to babysit. . . .

"Mother!" she pleaded. "Everybody's going minia-ture golfing! I told you that. I promised Tina and, and . . . " Desperately her mind searched for another reason. Anything. Any excuse would do. Then she had it. . . . "And Andy's even asked his mom to drive." Perfect! Bringing another adult into the picture always makes it sound more official.

For a moment there was silence as Sarah and her mom continued to set the table. Maybe Sarah had her. Maybe she'd actually convinced Mom to let her off the hook.

"I'd volunteer," Mom finally said, "if I hadn't al-ready promised to help out at the reception."

Sarah let out a long sigh. Sighing was some-thing she'd become an expert at. She wasn't sure when she'd gotten so good at it. Maybe it had had something to do with her fourteenth birthday. In any case, if they ever made sighing an Olympic event she'd be the one to bring home the gold.

"Sarah," Mom continued, "I'm not saying you have to do it, but . . . " She let the sentence hang there. That meant she wasn't going to lay down the law. It also meant if Sarah was really a decent, caring person she'd volunteer to help on her own.

It was an old trick, and Sarah saw through it. "Mom, don't 'guilt' me, OK?" She set the glasses on the table just a tad louder than normal before she crossed back to the counter.

"What time is the wedding?" Dad asked as he entered the room. He headed for the table and joined Nick and little Jamie. They were already sitting there—Jamie because she was waiting to eat and Nicholas because he was still doing his geography take-home quiz. Well, he really wasn't doing the quiz. He hadn't heard a word Mrs. Harmon had said during that last part of class. So he really couldn't answer the questions. Instead, he did the next best thing. He drew a map of the United States. Maybe that would help. Maybe she'd be impressed with his extra effort and give him a higher grade.

Mom joined Sarah back at the counter as she answered Dad. "The wedding's at two. And Sarah," she said, "I am not 'guilting' you. It's your decision."

Sarah quietly bit her lip. She hated it when that happened. She hated it when they left those types of decisions up to her. It was one thing to have your folks order you to do something. Then you could complain and grumble the whole time. But when they left the decision up to you . . . well, that was a whole other ball game. I mean, who could you complain and grumble against then?

It's not like she didn't want to help the Robinsons out. She knew how important it was for them to enjoy the wedding. But still she had all these great plans.

No way around it. It would be a tough decision—and she wasn't excited about making it. She wasn't sure what to do. So, she gave the best answer she knew. She let out another sigh.

Meanwhile, Nick glanced over to his little sister and asked her to pass him the milk.

" 'Pass the milk,' what?" Jamie asked. For some

reason manners were an important part of her life these days. It was time her big brother started learning a few.

Nick threw her a look. "Pass the milk, *please.*"

She passed it to him with a smile. She was pleased. For an older brother, he learned fast.

Sarah and Mom joined the rest of the family at the table. But as usual, Nick's stuff was spread out all over the place. More importantly, it was spread out all over Sarah's place.

"Nick," she snapped irritably. "Move your stupid books!"

Little Jamie, still thinking about manners, decided it was her big sister's turn to learn: " 'Move your stupid books,' *what?*" she asked.

Sarah looked at her. Then at Nicholas. Then at the ceiling.

She let out another sigh. . . .

THREE
Another Day, Another F

The next day at school Mrs. Harmon walked down the rows, passing back the geography quizzes. For some reason everyone was on their best behavior. Maybe it was because they'd suddenly become superpolite ladies and gentlemen. Maybe it was because they were suddenly very interested in geography. Or maybe, just maybe, it was because everyone had blown the quiz and wanted to get on Mrs. Harmon's good side again.

Nick had to smile. Silly children. Didn't they know it was too late for that now? If they really wanted to impress Mrs. Harmon, if they really wanted to get a better grade, they should have done extra credit. Like he did.

"Neat map," Mrs. Harmon said as she set the test on his desk.

Nick's smile turned into a grin. There was the map he had drawn, stapled to the front of the quiz. On it was a big happy face. The sign of a job well done. Yes sir, if anybody knew how to butter up teachers it was good ol' Nicholas Martin.

He casually reached for the map and turned it over to check out his grade on the quiz. Of course it would be an *A*. Maybe even an *A+*. He glanced down to the paper and there it was: *C+*.

C+!! Wait a minute! Didn't she see the map??

He looked up to her. For a moment he thought he caught a trace of a smile on her face as she moved down the aisle. Could it be? Could she really be that smart? Could the great teacher butter-upperer have finally met his match?

"Everyone," she asked the class. "What is the Continental Divide? Renee?"

Nick's friend was on the spot—but as usual she answered beautifully. "That's the dividing line in the Rockies where the river water flows east and west." She was so smart. He hated it.

"That's correct," Mrs. Harmon said as she continued passing out the quizzes.

Finally she came to a stop in front of Derrick Cryder's desk.

"Mr. Cryder," she said. "I have to say that of all the quiz papers, yours was the most . . . ," she searched for the word, " . . . creative."

Derrick, in all of his denseness, broke into a smug grin.

"Perhaps you'd share with the class your answer to number twenty-seven: What is the state capitol of Michigan?"

Derrick was caught off guard. He grabbed the test and quickly began to search for the answer he'd written. "Uhh . . . uhhh . . . " At last he found it. "Motown," he answered confidently.

The class broke into laughter. Motown was a famous record company, not a city.

Nick was laughing with the rest of them. It was a funny answer. But by the look on Derrick's face, being funny was not what he'd had in mind.

Mrs. Harmon wasn't done with him yet. "Number eight please . . . nice and loud. Where are the Great Plains located?"

Derrick's answer was a little weaker, a little less confident. "At the great airports?" he read.

Again the class broke out in laughter. Only this time it was much louder.

Derrick's face was turning red. His eyes were full of pain, embarrassment—and something else. They were also full of hate. And that hate was all directed toward one spot in the room. A little puzzled, Nick followed Derrick's death-look all the way across the room to, you guessed it, little Philip.

Uh-oh . . .

Philip didn't look so hot. In fact he looked kind of pale. Nick swallowed, suddenly feeling a little sick himself. Had the kid really decided to follow his suggestion? Had Phil really given Derrick all the wrong answers?

"Derrick . . ." It was Mrs. Harmon again. "If you want to waste your time here, that's up to you. But when you turn in a paper like this, you only cheat yourself."

A couple of the kids "ooo'd" to egg Derrick on. But Derrick wasn't paying attention. He was too busy drilling a hole into the back of Philip's head with his eyes. And Philip was too busy examining

31

his pencil, his shoes, the tile on the floor . . . anything to avoid meeting the bully's eyes.

"Oh, and Derrick," Mrs. Harmon concluded, "I want to see you after school."

Derrick threw a concerned look up to his teacher, but it was clear she had made up her mind. There would be no changing it. He was staying after school and that was that.

Nick watched as Derrick shot another icy stare over to Philip. Only this time Derrick caught Philip's eyes. Poor kid. He was frozen, unable to look away from the bully.

Slowly Derrick raised his paper so Philip could see. And there it was, scrawled across the front, the huge letter *F.*

Philip gave a weak, sickly smile.

Derrick didn't return it.

Nicholas felt terrible. How could he know the little guy was going to take him seriously? No one in their right mind would double-cross Derrick! Philip must have known Nick had only been kidding. He must have!

Philip continued to stare at Derrick . . . no doubt wondering where he could buy some quick, cheap health insurance.

Lunchtime finally came. But lunch at Nick's school was, well . . . have you ever seen those Wall Street guys on TV? Have you seen the way they holler and shout, and fight and bargain for the best deal? They look pretty tough, right? Well, those guys are nothing compared to the kids at Nick's lunch table.

Every day the kids made an art form of wheeling and dealing. Every day they traded corn chips for Fig Newtons, apples for bologna sandwiches, pudding cups for Hershey bars, raw vegetables for . . . well, usually there aren't any takers for raw vegetables. But I think you get the picture.

Today was no different.

"Half my chicken sandwich for your orange juice."

"What about your potato chips?"

"Fifty-fifty split."

"Sixty-forty and I'll give you seven Milk Duds."

"Deal!"

Then, just when all the trading was over, along came Renee, calling, "Jelly Donuts! I'm entertaining all serious offers!"

Suddenly a dozen lunches were shoved in her face, their owners pleading, whining, and begging for a trade.

It took a while but at last she made her deals. Nick was one of the lucky ones. He got a raspberry donut. Of course, he also got stuck with somebody's, uh . . . he took a peek. Oh no, how could anyone eat a cream cheese on datenut bread sandwich?? Oh well. At least he had the donut.

Before he bit into his prize Nicholas glanced up and saw Philip pass by. Normally everyone sits with their own group. The too-cools sit at one table, the jocks at another, and of course, the ultra-geeks way down at the far end. That's where Philip was heading—the far end.

But Nick was feeling a little sorry for him. So he

invited the kid to his table. Of course he had some other motives, too. "Hey, Philip. Got anything to trade for cream cheese on datenut bread? Yum!" It was Nicholas's best selling job, but Philip wasn't buying.

"Uh, no thanks," the boy said as he sat down across from him.

"Nicholas," Renee leaned over and whispered. "Why did you invite him to sit with us? He's weird."

Before Nick had a chance to answer, Derrick and a couple of his Dorks strolled up to the table.

"Hey, Philip." Derrick slapped his hand down hard on top of the boy's head. "Want to go to the airport and watch some great planes?" It was supposed to be a joke, but nobody was laughing. Not even Derrick. Then he saw the boy's lunch and grabbed it. "Think you're real funny, don't you?"

"Hey," Nick demanded. "Give Philip back his lunch!" Everyone at the table turned to Nicholas with surprise. Was he crazy talking to Derrick like that!? Didn't he know Derrick Cryder was famous for rearranging even the toughest kid's face? Funny thing was, Nick was just as surprised at his outburst as the rest of them. But the words had come out before he could stop them.

"Whose gonna make me, Martin?" Derrick sneered. "You?"

Nicholas swallowed hard. He'd gone too far. He knew there was nothing he could do to stop Derrick—at least not on his own. But if enough of them got together, Derrick wouldn't be able to touch Philip. If enough good, decent people stood up to the Derrick Cryders of the world, they'd just slither back under their rocks and leave everyone else alone. Yeah! That's the ticket—stand up to the bad guys and they'd have to back down.

And if ever there was time for a little 'standing up,' it was now.

"Look, Cryder," Nicholas said. His voice was a little shaky, but it grew stronger as he talked. "We're all sick and tired of the way you're picking on everybody." It sounded strong and heroic—just like John Wayne in one of those Saturday afternoon westerns on TV. Nick was pleased. He had shown courage. He had done his part. Now it was time for his friends to step in and join him in his courageous crusade. He turned to the rest of the table. "Isn't that right, guys?"

Nick waited for his pals to rise to their feet, join together, and shout, "That's right partner! We ain't puttin' up with that ornery good-fer-nothin' sidewinder no more!" Instead, each of the kids suddenly looked away, or began to wonder what was in his lunch bag, what her sandwich was made of, or if any food had fallen under the table.

Derrick looked on with a smirk. No way would these wimps stand up to him. Not the fearsome Derrick Cryder. Then Derrick spotted Nick's donut. He reached out and quickly grabbed it. "Mmmm. A jelly donut. I wonder what flavor it is?" Suddenly he squashed the donut down hard on top of Philip's head.

The Dorks doubled over in laughter.

Immediately Nicholas was on his feet. "Aw, come on! That's enough!" But Derrick barely heard. Instead he just stood there grinning as he watched

35

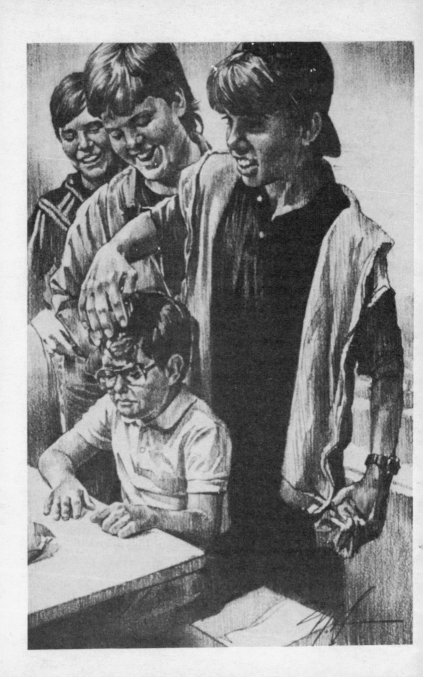

the red goop slowly ooze down Philip's head, over his eyebrows, and onto his glasses.

"Hmm, raspberry," Derrick chuckled. "My favorite."

Nick continued to stand, facing the bully. Maybe the other kids would join him now. Maybe they'd seen enough. Maybe they'd all stand up and finally put a stop to Derrick Cryder.

Then again, maybe not . . .

Derrick turned to them with a sneer and taunted, "Anyone else wanna donate to the cause?"

No one moved a muscle. No one said a word. They just kept staring at their lunches—hoping they wouldn't become the next victim.

Derrick grinned. He had them and he knew it. He was in control. They were too scared to do anything. That's the way it had always been and that's the way it would stay.

He turned back to Philip. "Oh, here Dude. You can have your lunch." He held it out for Philip. But as the boy reached to grab it Derrick dropped it on the ground.

More laughter from the Dorks.

For a moment Philip wasn't sure what he should do. Should he reach down and pick it up or should he just stay put until Derrick was gone?

The bully helped him make up his mind. He hit Philip on the side of the head so hard that it knocked him off of the bench and onto the ground.

Nick wanted to move. He wanted to help. But something stopped him. Maybe it was his fear of death.

As a final act of cruelty, Derrick's big high top

crunched down on top of Philip's lunch, pulverizing it into the dirt. "The fun's just started, Nerd," he growled. With that Derrick and his thugs strolled off, laughing.

For a moment Nicholas just stood there. He couldn't believe what had happened. Why hadn't he done something? Why hadn't Louis and Renee offered to help?

He crossed around the table to help Philip sit up. The little guy's face was smeared with jelly. Although he tried to be brave, there was no missing the tears starting to run down his little cheeks.

Nicholas felt the anger start to grow inside of him. It came from somewhere deep inside his chest. But he wasn't just angry at Derrick. He was was also angry at his friends. And at himself.

This was the second time he had sat back and watched Philip get hurt. First, when he hid behind the wall when Philip was mugged. Now this time. Sure, he had stood up and said something. But why hadn't he moved in and actually *done* something?

The question bugged him through the rest of the day. It bugged him through dinner. And later, up in his room, it bugged him at his drawing table.

FOUR
The Challenge

Jesus replied with an illustration: "A Jew going on a trip from Jerusalem to Jericho was attacked by bandits. They stripped him of his clothes and money and beat him up and left him lying half dead beside the road. By chance a Jewish priest came along; and when he saw the man lying there, he crossed to the other side of the road and passed him by. A Jewish temple-assistant walked over and looked at him lying there, but then went on. But a despised Samaritan came along, and when he saw him, he felt deep pity. Kneeling beside him the Samaritan soothed his wounds with medicine and bandaged them. Then he put the man on his donkey and walked along beside him till they came to an inn, where he nursed him through the night.

"The next day he handed the innkeeper two twenty-dollar bills and told him to take care of the man. 'If his bill runs higher than that,' he said, 'I'll pay the difference the next time I am here.'

"Now," Jesus asked, "which of these three would you say was a neighbor to the bandits' victim?"

The man replied, "The one who showed him some pity."

Then Jesus said, "Yes, now go and do the same." (Luke 10:30-37, *The Living Bible*)

Old Nick let out a long sigh. It was almost as good as one of Sarah's. We'd been at his drawing table for over an hour. But I could tell that reading this Bible story and sketching me as it's superhero wasn't enough. Nick knew God wanted him to do something else. All we had to do was figure out what.

I mean, what more could God expect? Hadn't Nick shown Philip enough love? After all, he gave him that nice post-mugging pep talk. And what about letting him sit at our lunch table? Or Nick's speech to Derrick? And let's not forget his offer of the ever-popular datenut and cream cheese sandwich. I mean, how much love could one guy give?

The answer that kept seeming to come back to Nick was just one word: More.

Finally, in desperation, he turned to me. A smart move since I always have an answer to everything. (It may not always be the right answer, but at least it's an answer.) "So what am I supposed to do against Derrick and the goon platoon?" he asked.

"Do" was my cue. I mean, if there is anything I can do it's do. So that's what I did. I dood . . . uh, did. I took center stage and laid out the facts. "You

can call Goliath-breath out, that's what. One-on-one, man-to-man, mano-a-mano—"

"Victim-to-mugger," Nick interrupted.

I wasn't listening. Not to Nick, anyway. Actually, I was listening to the theme from "Rocky" which started in my head as I began to practice my boxing. Already I could see the lights and hear the crowd as they started to chant "Mc-Gee, Mc-Gee, Mc-Gee."

I began dancing around the desk, sparring with my opponent Pink Peril, the Eraser. "I see it all now," I shouted to Nick between jabs. "You get him against the ropes. He comes at you like a Mack truck! He swings, you duck."

Suddenly I landed an upper cut that sent ol' Pinky to the moon.

"McGee," he groaned as he reached out and caught the flying eraser. "The guy's almost twice my size. Besides, you know how Mom and Dad feel about fighting."

Suddenly the lights were gone, the crowd was silent. Nick was right.

"A-ha, I've got it!" Now I was in my Three Musketeer outfit—complete with flowing cape and feathered hat. "Challenge the ne'er-do-well to a duel!" I shouted.

I pulled out my sword and began to fence. First forward, then backward, then forward again. I hadn't invented an opponent yet, but hey, who needs an opponent. It's not whether you win or lose that counts, it's how great your clothes fit. And mine looked great! "Challenge him to plastic swords at high noon!" I said. "Or eleven o'clock central time, whichever comes first."

"A duel?" Nick questioned.

"Yeah. En garde!" I continued my imaginary swordplay, dancing backward and forward with breathtaking agility. "Ha ha! Take that, you cur! For the underdog! For mom and apple pie! For season tickets to the opera! For—" I did a marvelous leap backwards . . . right into one of Nick's sharpest pencils. "YeeOWWWWWWWWWWWW!"

Needless to say I got the point. (I also set a new record in the high jump while practically screaming my lungs out in the process.) Finally I came to rest on the giant pencil over Nick's desk. Or at least my cape came to rest there. Actually it was caught— and since I was attached to it I really didn't have much choice but to just sort of, you know, hang around.

Nick shook his head. "Cute, McGee."

Instead of basking in all of the sympathy he was dishing out, I looked around, scoping out my situation. Suddenly, I found the answer to Nick's problem. "That's it!" I called. "I have found yon solution! 'Tis brrrrilliant!"

"What now? Sumo wrestling?"

"Nope." I pointed to the photo right below me on the desk. It was Nick with his skateboard. "This'll be so easy, you can just 'skate' through it." I gave him a wink. "Get it?"

"Quit clowning," Nick said as he reached for the picture. It was a pretty good photo even though I wasn't in it. It was of Nick, holding his skateboard.

But there was more to the photo than just the

42

photo. And as I looked at Nick I could see in his eyes
that his little mind was starting to turn . . . that he al-
ready was starting to see a "bigger" picture. . . .

The next morning, Nicholas stood by the front of
the school. The rest of the kids passed by, talking
and sharing the latest gossip on their way to class.
Not Nick. He just stood there, waiting. Oh, and he
also did a little wondering. Like how many
minutes he had left to live.

You guessed it. Nicholas was waiting to talk
with Derrick. Something he looked forward to
about as much as getting a root canal (which
might be a lot less painful). Still, after reading the
Bible with McGee the night before, Nick knew he
had to do something more for Philip.

"Hi, Nick." It was Renee. She had just gotten off
the bus with Louis and was heading up the
sidewalk. "What are you doing out here? You're
going to be late."

"Yeah, who you waiting for?" Louis asked.

"Uh, nobody special . . . "

The kids gave a shrug and started up the steps.

"Just Derrick Cryder."

Immediately they did a U-turn and came back
to join Nicholas. They weren't sure why their
friend was thinking of suicide, but they figured it
wouldn't hurt to stick around and catch the action.

Before Nick had a chance to explain, Louis
glanced across the street. "Looks like you got your
wish," he said.

Derrick and a couple of his want-ta-be hoods
stepped into the street without bothering to look.

A station wagon slammed on its brakes and swerved to avoid hitting them. It missed Derrick by only a few feet, but Derrick didn't notice. He expected the world to stop for him—and it usually did. Especially around the school, where the kids were all a couple years younger (and a good half-foot shorter) than he was.

Nick swallowed. *Here goes nothing,* he thought. He took a breath and shouted, "Hey Derrick!" His voice sounded strong and determined. So far so good. "I want to talk to you!"

The bully's head snapped around in Nick's direction. Was it just Nick's imagination or was a sneer already starting to break across Derrick's thin, rubbery lips?

As they approached, Louis had an idea. He was a great thinker and always liked to plan in advance. "Hey, why don't I just run ahead and tell the nurse to get out the bandages?"

Before Nick could answer, Derrick was there. In his usual courteous manner, he politely snarled, "What'd you say, Wimp?"

Out of the corner of his eye Nicholas could see other kids start to gather around. Well, it was now or never. . . .

"I want . . . ," his voice cracked and sort of disappeared.

Derrick's sneer grew bigger. He could tell Nick was as scared of him as everyone else was.

Nicholas cleared his voice and tried again. "I want to settle this thing between you and Philip."

A faint gasp escaped from the crowd.

Derrick was no longer sneering. The sneer had

turned into a grin. A huge grin. What was wrong with this kid, anyway? He actually *wanted* to fight him . . . him, Derrick-the-Destroyer, Derrick-the-Demolisher, Derrick-the-Devastater. Well, far be it from Derrick to deprive anyone out of that wish. Besides, he loved slugfests.

"All right!" Derrick chuckled. "You're on! At the flagpole after school."

"No, not a fight." Nicholas interrupted.

Derrick's grin started to fade.

"A race," Nick continued. "This Saturday. Skateboard-to-skateboard. You lose, you have to lay off of Philip."

"And what happens when you lose . . . like you're gonna?" Derrick said, sneering.

For a moment Nick was stumped. Losing had never entered his mind. Then one of Derrick's Dorks spoke up. "Hey I got it. Make him be your slaaaaave!"

Derrick's grin returned. Not a bad idea. Why hadn't he thought of it? "Yeah," he said, his grin widening. "For a week."

Now the ball was in Nick's court. A slave? To Derrick Cryder? For a whole week? It wasn't exactly his idea of a good time. But, hey, that was only if he lost. And there was no way he could lose. Not Nicholas Martin. Not when he was on a skateboard.

"All right," Nick nodded. "You're on."

Derrick broke into another little laugh. "OK, you got it, Twerp." He gave Nicholas a shove and headed for the steps. "Later . . ."

The Dorks followed, laughing and yukking it up.

"You're dead meat," one of them shouted to Nick, "Hamburger!"

The threats didn't bother Nicholas. He was feeling good. Better than good—he was feeling great. He had stood up to the dreaded Derrick Cryder and hadn't backed down. What's more he had Derrick right where he wanted him . . . on a skateboard. Glowing with pride over a job well done, he turned to Louis and Renee. No doubt some back-slapping and "atta-boy-Nick"s would be in order.

But they just stared at him, shaking their heads. Finally Louis spoke up, and he looked anything but pleased. "Bad news, Nick."

"Do you know what you're doing?" Renee asked.

"Sure I do," Nick grinned. "I can beat him, no sweat."

More silence. Louis just kept on shaking his head. "No way, man," he said. "Derrick won third place last year in the Tri-City finals. He'll smear you."

For a moment Nicholas thought he was kidding. But the look on Louis's face made it clear this was no laughing matter.

Oh no! Why hadn't somebody told him? Why hadn't they warned him? Third place? Tri-City finals!? Nick wasn't that good. He'd *never* be that good!

After another moment of mournful silence, Louis and Renee turned and started for the school. Nick was all alone. What had gone wrong? What had happened? Here he was trying to do the right thing, trying to help Philip like God wanted him to, and now look what happened!

I mean, what did God expect from him, anyway? How much love was he supposed to dish out?

He let out a long sigh and headed for the steps. It was going to be one very long week. . . .

FIVE
The Decision

Blurp . . . beep, beep, beep, beep.

Silently my mini-sub cut through the dark, treacherous waters.

Blurp . . . beep, beep, beep, beep.

My gorgeous baby blues peered through the portholes as the eyes of only a trained professional can peer. I saw nothing. The thick blackness outside swallowed up my searchlights, making them about as useful as a squirt gun in a forest fire. No, better make that a surfboard in the Sahara. OK, how 'bout five dollars at a shopping mall?

Blurp . . . beep, beep, beep, beep.

All I had to go on was my sonar. It blurped and beeped, guiding me across the ocean floor. But it didn't tell me what I already knew . . . there was something out there.

For the third time in two weeks a giant oil tanker had been ripped apart at this very location, spilling its black goo into our precious environment. That's why the water was so dark and murky. And that's why they called on me . . . California Clyde, world-famous explorer, adventurer, and Uno player.

Blurp . . . beep, beep, beep, POOOING!

"Poooing?" That could only mean one thing! CONTACT! I knew it. There was something out there! I threw the turbo-thrusters into "Lickety-Split" and began pursuit.

Blurp . . . beep, beep, POOOING!

Closer and closer I came.

Blurp . . . beep, POOOING!

Blurp . . . POOOING!

POOOING! POOOING! POOOING!

Holy heart attack! I was right on top of him . . . it . . . whatever. Quickly I snapped on the outside TV cameras to see what was there. Oh no! Could it be? Why, that looked just like Marsha Brady on my screen. And there was her little sister Cindy, and their cook Alice, and—oh no—the brothers too! The whole Brady Bunch gang was in on it. How could this be? They were such sweet kids—how could they have gotten involved in this tanker-wrecking business?

I was brokenhearted. Then an idea crossed my mind. In a flash of genius I reached over and changed channels.

There, that was better. Now I could see the ocean floor, the murky water, and . . . Great Scott! It was impossible, but true. It was the fabled and notorious Locknose Monster! And it was coming right at me!

I threw my turbo thrusters into "Let's-Get-Outta-Here-and-Fast," but I was too late. The monster grabbed the sub with its iron jaws and began to shake my little sub back and forth like a puppy with an old slipper. I looked out my porthole, but all I could see were a pair of gigantic molars that looked like they'd missed their annual dental check-up by a couple dozen centuries.

For years everyone thought the Locknose Monster was a myth, a fairy tale. But by the way I was about to lose my cookies from all this shaking and bouncing, I could tell ol' beasty boy here was no myth.

I reached for my phaser button and fired a good blast. Phhsssst-BLAM!

The beast threw open his mouth in a ferocious howl of anger. I would have loved to stick around. You know, talk about old times, look at some home videos of his little grandmonsters. But I figured he wasn't in the mood. So I said a hasty good-bye and split.

Desperately I sped for the surface. He was right behind me. Poor, lonely guy. He obviously didn't want to see me go just yet. Still, I hate long good-byes, so the sooner I got to shore the better.

At last my sub reached the surface and I popped open the hatch . . . only to be met by a huge downpour of oil. It came crashing in, sending my poor little mini-sub tumbling and twirling out of control. I leaped for my life and swam to the nearby shore. It was tough going in the thick gooey gunk, but at last I made it to the edge of the oil pan. That's right, "oil pan." Breathing hard, I finally looked up to see Nick's dad. He was directly overhead changing the oil in the family's car—draining all the old stuff into my make-believe ocean.

*It was one of my messier fantasies. I wasn't too
thrilled about being covered in all that oily gunk.
But I gave a shrug and pulled myself out of the
pan. I guess it would take a little more practice
before I got the hang of it. After that, who knows.
Beware Indiana Jones, California Clyde is on his
way. Well, OK. Not yet. He has to take a shower
first. Uh, better make that two or three showers.*

Nick's dad looked up from working on the car. "So
you're going to give up, then?" he asked Nick,
wiping his hands on a nearby rag.

For nearly an hour the two of them had been
talking while they worked on the car in the garage.
Actually, Dad was the one doing the work.
Nicholas was the one doing the talking. It didn't
start out that way, but before Nick knew it he had
told Dad all about Derrick, the race, and everything.

"The guy came in third at the Tri-City finals,"
Nicholas moaned. "He'll cream me!"

"Probably," Dad agreed. "Hand me the crescent
wrench, there." Nicholas reached over and handed
him the wrench. "So tell me, what's going to happen to your friend, Philip?"

Nick let out a heavy sigh. He'd been so worried
about becoming Derrick's slave that he hadn't
even thought of Philip. "Haven't I done enough for
him? I mean, first I helped out after the little mug-
ging with Derrick and the Dorks. Then I let him sit
at our lunch table. And I even tried to stand up for
him . . . a couple of times."

"That's great, Nick. Good for you." Dad stuck his

head back under the hood and seemed to disappear somewhere inside the engine.

Nicholas wasn't sure what his dad was up to. Maybe he wasn't paying that much attention. Or maybe he already had the answer but just wanted Nick to do a little thinking on his own.

"I've done enough, right?" Nick asked. There was no answer. Just a lot of grunting from under the hood. "Right, Dad? . . . Dad?"

Finally Dad answered. "That depends," he said from somewhere under the hood. After a few more grunts, he continued. "I mean, Jesus asked us to love our neighbors as much as he loves us."

"So?" Nicholas asked.

"So . . . I guess the question is how much love would Jesus show Philip?"

"Jesus didn't have to face the Tri-City Terror on a skateboard."

"That's true. All he had to do was put up with being beaten, spit on, tortured, and killed."

Nicholas took a deep breath. "That's a lot of love."

"You can say that again . . . Ouch!" The wrench clattered and clanked to the ground—followed by a small bolt. "Doggone it," Dad said as he pulled his head out of the hood. He was sucking his skinned knuckles.

Nick was used to that sort of thing. I mean, when it came to being a great man of wisdom nobody was better than his dad. When it came to being a great man with tools . . . well, that was another story. More like a horror story.

But Nicholas wasn't thinking about that. His

mind was still back on what his dad had said.
How much love *would* Jesus show? "You know,"
Nick said as he dropped to his knees to help look
for the bolt. "That race isn't for a few more days. I
suppose if I practiced real hard . . . well, I might
have a *slight* chance of beating Derrick."

Dad said nothing as they continued to search
for the bolt.

"I mean, it'd be a *very* slight chance."

The search continued.

"But I suppose a slight chance is better than no
chance at all. Isn't it?"

More silence. For some reason Dad wasn't
saying anything. But that didn't seem to matter.
Nick was already making up his mind. "I mean, I
should at least give it a try, shouldn't I? For
Philip?"

Still more silence. Then . . . "Ah, here it is," Dad
picked up the bolt and rose to his feet.

Nicholas was already standing. His decision was
made. He started toward the door.

"Hey, where are you going?" Dad called. "I
thought we were going to work on this car."

"I'd love to. But the race is the day after tomorrow. If I don't start training now I won't have a
chance. Do you mind?"

"If you have to," Dad muttered gruffly. "Go
ahead."

"Thanks," Nick grinned as he disappeared out
the door.

If he'd stayed just a second longer he would
have seen a similar grin break across Dad's face.
A grin that said Mr. Martin was proud of his son.

And a grin that said he had been listening to every word of the conversation and had known all along what Nick should—and eventually would—do.

Still grinning, he stuck his head back under the hood of the car, content that Nick was on his way to winning his "loving-others-like-God-loves-'em" battle. What neither Dad nor Nick knew, though, was that there was a similar battle going on with another member of the family.

Nick had his skateboard on the kitchen counter, adjusting the wheels. Just then Sarah and her friend Andy came in and made their usual beeline for the fridge.

Andy was a pretty good guy. Friendly, athletic, and popular. Very popular. In fact he was vice-president of his class. Ever since the Martins had moved to town Sarah had been trying to be Andy's friend. Not because she was interested in him as a boyfriend or anything like that. It was because he was part of the "in" group, the popular group. Being popular was very important to Sarah . . . maybe too important.

For months she'd been working to get into Andy's group. It was a long, slow process of being seen with the right people at the right time. Being nice to this person. (Being mean to that person.) But finally it was starting to pay off.

First the girls from the group began talking to her in the halls. Then they began inviting her to eat lunch at their table. And now, after all her months of hard work, Sarah was about to receive her reward—the real proof that she was in. The group had invited her to play miniature golf with them this Saturday!

Fantastic! Terrific! Wonderful! Well, not quite. There was still that little item of whether or not Sarah was going to babysit for the Robinsons during their niece's wedding . . . this Saturday.

"Look," Andy reasoned. "Your mom said you didn't have to babysit."

"Yeah, so?" Sarah said as she grabbed a root-beer from the fridge and handed it to him. The "in" group always drank rootbeer.

"So, if you don't want to do it, don't."

It sounded simple enough. But what about the Robinsons? What about them having a miserable time at their niece's wedding because no one would look after their four-year-old? What about Mom trusting Sarah to make the right decision? Sarah wanted to explain all this, but she knew she wouldn't be any good at putting it into words. So she did something she was good at. She snapped at Nicholas.

"Don't let Mom catch you working on the counter!"

"Hey, Nick." Sarah looked at Andy in surprise as he sauntered up to her little brother. "How's it going?"

Suddenly Sarah was in a panic. What if Nicholas said something stupid . . . like he always did. What if he said something to embarrass her. She tried to catch his eye, to signal him—to say in one look that she was sorry for everything she'd ever done to him and if he promised to behave and keep his mouth shut she would be his slave forever and until the end of time.

He never saw the look.

"Hi, Andy."

Sarah covered her eyes. This was going to be awful.

Andy continued. "My brother Patrick told me about your big race. Pretty tough stuff. You up to it?"

"Yeah, I hope," Nick said as he laid down the wrench.

Sarah peeked through her fingers, puzzled. What gave? No jokes about her messy bedroom? No jabs about the hours she spends in front of the bathroom mirror? Not even a comment about her smelly socks? What was wrong? Was little brother not feeling well?

Finally Nick grabbed his skateboard and started out of the room.

"Good luck Saturday," Andy called after him.

"Thanks, I'm gonna need it," Nick said with a slight smile as he left.

Sarah stared after her brother in amazement. What had come over him? Why was he so kind?

"That's a cool thing your brother's doing." Andy said as he took a huge gulp of pop. "Not many people go out of their way to help someone else."

Sarah gave a weak little nod. Nick was cool, all right. Not only in the way he'd kept his mouth shut about her, but also in what he was doing for Philip. *Amazing*, Sarah thought. Then another thought came to her mind . . .

Could *she* be that cool? About the Robinsons?

Could she sacrifice the miniature golf game and risk falling out of the "in" group? Could she show that kind of love?

Once again Sarah Martin let out one of her world-famous sighs. . . .

SIX
Blood, Sweat, and Fears

Nicholas got home from school at 3:20 every afternoon. The next day, at 3:21, Philip was sitting on
his steps. There was lots of work to do between
now and the race, and Philip wanted to be there to
help. After all, he had even more at stake than
Nicholas.

Finally the front door opened and Nick appeared. He was covered head to foot in knee pads,
elbow pads, and a helmet. He wasn't taking any
chances. It'd been a long time since he'd skated in
competition and the last thing he needed was a
broken arm or leg . . . or head.

Philip was on his feet and at Nick's side in a
shot. "I got something for you."

"What's that?"

"It's for the race." Carefully Philip unfolded a
beautiful blue shirt. Scrawled across the front in
rad, bold lettering was the word *SKATE!*

For a moment Nick was kind of floored. It wasn't
like the kid had given him a sports car or CD

player or anything like that. It was just surprising that Philip would go to all that trouble to buy Nick a shirt. Even more surprising was the look in Philip's eyes. A look that said, "You're a great guy, Nicholas Martin, and I'm really glad you're help-ing."

"Thanks, Philip. . . ." was about all Nick could say.

The kid gave an embarrassed shrug. Nicholas had to smile. There was a warmth starting to glow somewhere inside his chest. It wasn't real notice-able, but it was there. This love business wasn't so bad. Not only did he have an incredible glow in-side, but, hey, he had a new shirt. A shirt they just might have to bury him in if he didn't get to practicing. "Come on," Nick said as he started down the stairs. "Let's get to work!"

Philip gave a nod and followed.

Meanwhile Derrick was experiencing his own kind of "glow." The glow that comes from skating down the sidewalk so fast you know no one will be able to touch you. The glow that comes to bad guys when they know they're going to destroy the good guys.

"All right! Way to go!" the Dorks cried as he zoomed past them.

Derrick slid to a stop, a smug smile on his face. Nicholas Martin was history.

It was Louis's job to set up the race course. No one knew where it would be or what type of obstacles he would put in it. That was a surprise. But know-

60

ing Louis, it would be good. And, knowing Louis's honesty, neither Nick nor Derrick would find out anything about the course until they got there.

Still, nearly all race courses have slaloms. So that's what Nicholas and Philip worked on first. They borrowed some garbage cans from the neighbors and set them up and down the sidewalk. Nick was suppose to weave in and out of them on his board as quickly as he could. No problem. He'd done it a million times before. But for some reason today was different. Maybe it was the tension. Or maybe it was going seven months without being on a board. Whatever the reason, well . . . let's just say it wasn't a pretty sight.

His first attempt looked like he was trying to knock down as many cans as he could.

The second time wasn't much better.

By the third try he was starting to get the hang of it. Only two or three cans bit the dust. He was feeling a little better . . . until he looked at the time on Philip's stopwatch. Too slow. Way too slow. He shook his head and headed back to the starting line again. It was going to be a long afternoon.

Over at the park, Derrick couldn't have been hotter. In fact he was so good he began to wonder why he even bothered to practice. Sure, the race was tomorrow; but when you're as good as he was, what's the point? To pass time Derrick began showing off for his goon-patrol—doing boardwalks, ollies, rollos. You name it, he did it . . . and he did it beautifully.

Again Nicholas tried the slalom. Too slow. So he tried again. Still too slow. And again . . . well, I think you get the picture. Finally, for a change of pace, Philip suggested he try a few ollies.

"Louis isn't going to put any ollies in the course, is he?" Nicholas asked weakly. An "ollie" is a move where you and your skateboard have to jump over something together. By the tone in Nick's voice it was a pretty safe guess that ollies were not his strongest event.

Unfortunately, Philip thought Louis might throw in a few. So Nicholas reluctantly gave in and started to work on them. As you can imagine, an ollie isn't easy to do—but Nick could handle the small ones. At least, he used to be able to handle them. Unfortunately, he was about to discover that as bad as his slaloms were, they looked tremendous compared to his ollies.

The two boys grabbed the trash bin Nick's mom kept in the kitchen (they were getting quite a collection of trash containers) and set it on its side in the middle of the sidewalk. Nick took a deep breath, hopped on his skateboard, and came roaring at the trash bin full tilt. He needed every ounce of concentration and skill that he had. Unfortunately, that wasn't quite enough. He came to the bin and lifted off the ground beautifully. There was nothing wrong with the lift-off. It was great. The fall-down, on the other hand, went a little haywire. Without getting into the gory details, just picture Nick flat on his back in the middle of the sidewalk, staring up at the sky, with his skateboard resting upside down on his chest (the

wheels still spinning). Suddenly he was very grateful he'd worn his helmet and pads.

Immediately Philip was at his side "Maybe we should go back to the slalom," he suggested weakly.

Nick didn't answer. Mainly because at the moment he couldn't answer. Philip waited nervously. He could see Nick was still breathing and that he had his eyes open. He could also see that his newfound hero wasn't doing a lot of moving. Maybe Nick just wasn't cut out for the hero business. . . .

Finally Nicholas rolled onto his stomach. Then slowly he got to his knees. One of these days he knew the sidewalk would stop spinning around and maybe—just maybe—the pain would go away. But none of that really concerned him right now. Instead, a question had started to grow in his mind. It had started out as just a tiny whisper. After that last fall, though, it was a lot louder: *Is all this worth it? All this pain, all this work?* When you thought about it, what had Philip ever done for Nick? Sure, he gave him a shirt—but big deal. Anybody could buy a stupid shirt.

Nicholas raised his head to take a look at Philip. The kid wasn't much. Just a shrimp with glasses. He didn't even have a decent personality. No wonder Derrick picked on him. No wonder the kids avoided him. So would somebody mind explaining what he, Nicholas Martin, was doing trying to help this loser and probably getting killed in the process?

Then Nick noticed the look in Philip's eyes. *Oh no you don't. Just forget it,* he thought. *Don't play that helpless puppy stuff with me.*

But Philip wasn't playing helpless. In fact, his eyes were full of hope and trust. Hope that Nicholas was OK. Trust that he wouldn't let him down.

Then if that weren't bad enough, Nick began to hear the voice of his dad. "It all depends," he heard him say. "How much love would Jesus show Philip?"

Nick took a deep breath. He had his answer. Sure, Philip was a wimp and a shrimp. But he was a wimpy shrimp Jesus loved. If Jesus loved this kid enough to suffer and die for him then who was Nick to think he wasn't worth the effort?

Don't get me wrong. It wasn't like Nicholas suddenly had this wonderful feeling of love toward the kid. To be honest, he still didn't feel like helping Philip. But there on his knees on the sidewalk— his body aching, his head spinning—he began to realize there was a different type of love.

It wasn't a love that gave you warm feelings inside. It really had nothing to do with feelings. Instead it had to do with obedience. It was a love that said, "I'll love you regardless of what I'm feeling," . . . and "I'll love you because Jesus did—because that's what he wants me to do."

Slowly Nicholas rose to his feet.

Philip watched him, worry and concern all over his face.

Finally Nick looked down to him. He tried to smile, but he hurt too much. Instead he gave the guy a little pat on the shoulder, grabbed his board and slowly limped toward the starting line. He was going to work on that ollie until he got it right.

Over and over again he tried. And over and over again he failed. But each time he failed a little less. Then . . .

Nicholas stood at the starting line and looked down the sidewalk at the trash bin. The heat off the cement made it shimmer in the sun. He glanced over to Philip who was standing right beside it, looking on, hoping.

Nick set the board down and looked back to the bin. Then after a deep breath he hoped on and pushed off. He'd wiped out so many times that his bruises were getting bruises. But he wasn't going to let that psych him out. He had to treat each time like it was the first—like he hadn't crashed at all.

Nick could feel the board vibrate under his feet as he got closer and closer to the bin. He never took his eyes off the bin. Finally he was there. It was time. He kicked the tail of the board down. As soon as the nose rose he gave a little hop. The board stayed with his feet. Perfect. Now he was weightless and soaring. But that was only the beginning. Now he had to push the board down with his front foot to keep it balanced. That was the tricky part. For a moment he went too far. He felt himself lurching forward and to the left. Any moment he'd be in another fiery crash. But he wouldn't give up. He wouldn't quit. He fought extra hard, struggling to the very last second to get his balance. And . . . he landed beautifully!

"All right!!" Philip raced to him and they high-fived. "You did it! You did it!" Philip hollered in excitement, dancing around.

Nicholas was excited, too. He just didn't show it. He was too tired to show it. Besides, they still had to work on the slalom.

And work they did. . . .

It was over an hour before Nick was able to cut the time down closer to what he wanted. Philip suggested they quit. After all, Nick was beat and it was getting dark. But Nicholas wanted to give it one last shot. He had to. He had to be in top shape for tomorrow.

One last time he stood at the starting line and concentrated on the sidewalk in front of him. For a second he thought he caught something out of the corner of his eye. But he paid no attention. It was just him and the slalom.

Had he paid attention, he would have seen something that might have ruined his day. He would have seen Derrick and his Dorks watching from around the corner.

Nicholas pushed off and took the slalom beautifully. Every move was perfect. The board responded exactly as it should. He really felt like it was a part of his body now. He roared past each trash can, passing so close he could feel the wind from them. But he didn't touch them. Not a one. At last, he raced across the finish line where Philip was standing. He'd nailed it! He knew he'd beat the time! He knew it!

The little guy raced up to him and couldn't help but throw his arms around him. "We did it, Nicholas!" he squeaked, showing him the time on the stopwatch. "We did it!!" Finally Nick had to smile. He couldn't help it.

He might not have been smiling, though, if he'd seen the look on Derrick's face.

"Not bad," one of Dorks said.

Derrick quietly nodded his head. There was a long moment before he finally spoke. "We better fix him, just to be sure." Another pause and then he finished, "Fix him good."

The Dorks knew exactly what Derrick meant. They didn't have much time before the race. But one thing was for certain: They would fix Nicholas Martin—they would fix him "good."

SEVEN
T Minus One Night . . . and Counting

No one had to tell Nick to go to bed that night. He was beat, but it was the type of beat that felt good. The type of beat that told him, "You did all right, kid."

Before he crawled into bed, Nicholas picked up his new skate shirt. But he barely saw it. Instead, he was seeing the look in Philip's eyes when he'd given Nick the shirt. OK, this love stuff was tough. No doubt about it. But it was also good . . . very good.

He laid the shirt down and crossed over to his bed. The skateboard sat there on its side. It was only a few days old, but it already looked like it had been through a couple of wars. After today's workout, it had.

He plopped on the bed and reached for the board. It had a nice balance, a great feel. He gave the wheels a spin. They seemed to roll forever. Yes sir, this board had everything he needed. Everything except the skill. That had to come from Nick.

Did he have enough? A worried look came

69

across his face. Did he really have enough skill to pull it off?

Nicholas placed the board on the floor. As he sat there thinking he quietly rolled it back and forth with his feet.

What was it McGee had said? *"This'll be so easy, you can just 'skate' through it."*

Yeah, well, not quite.

Then he heard Louis's voice: *"Third place at the Tri-City Finals . . . He'll smear you."* Nicholas swallowed hard. Louis's comment stayed in his brain. It wouldn't go away.

After a moment Nick gave the board a gentle push with his foot. It rolled slowly across the room and came to a stop. He stared at it a long time, thinking, remembering . . .

"Do you know what you're doing?"

"Sure I do . . . I can beat him."

But Nick wasn't so sure. *Could* he beat Derrick? Really, honestly . . . did he even stand a chance? He threw the covers back and crawled between the sheets. They felt crisp and cool against his tired legs. He reached for the Voice-Activated-Light-Turner-Offer (one of his many ingenious inventions). He gave a low whistle. The light turned off.

Unfortunately his mind didn't.

Nick stared up at the ceiling, watching the strange shadows the moonlight and the tree outside made on it. But he paid no attention. He was too busy listening to the voices in his head.

"And what happens when you lose, like you're gonna?" It was Derrick this time. He was right. What *would* happen?

"You're dead meat, man." Of course it was one of the Dorks now. Well, maybe the kid was right. Maybe Nick would be dead meat.

The thoughts kept coming. Nick tried to force them out of his mind but as soon as he pushed one out, another crept in from the other side. So he just kept lying there, staring at the shadows on the ceiling, listening to all the voices. It didn't seem to matter what he did, he couldn't stop them. Nor could he stop the battle going on in his head.

Downstairs on the phone, Sarah was having her own little battle.

"Andy says you might not go miniature golfing with us tomorrow?" It was her friend, Tina, on the other end. *Amazing how good news travels fast,* Sarah thought to herself.

"I didn't say that," she protested. "It's just that there's this wedding and—"

"Good," Tina broke in. " 'Cause I went to a lot of trouble to get you invited."

"Right, and I—"

"This is your big chance to be in the group. Don't blow it."

"Yeah . . . ," Sarah said as she shifted her weight on the vinyl kitchen stool. Suddenly it felt very sticky and uncomfortable.

"Listen, my dad wants to use the phone again," Tina said. "He can be such a bother. See you around two, OK? 'Bye."

Before Sarah had a chance to answer Tina had hung up. Tina did a lot of that—asking questions without waiting for answers.

" 'Bye," Sarah said to the empty line. She sat there a long time, listening to the dial tone. Then slowly she hung up the receiver.

What was she going to do?

Upstairs, the voices and memories were still roaring inside Nicholas's head. He couldn't get to sleep. Then, finally, something came to mind. Nick wondered why he hadn't thought of it before.

He closed his eyes. Quietly he began to pray. "I'm not sure if I can beat Derrick, Lord. Maybe I can't." He thought about that for a long time. Maybe he would get creamed. Maybe he would get destroyed. Then slowly something began to dawn on him.

Sure, winning was important. Make no mistake about it. But there seemed to be something even more important than the winning. It was that very something that had gotten him into all of this in the first place. It was that something called "love." Real love. God's love. That's what this whole thing was really about: loving someone because God tells you to. When it was all said and done, that's really all Nick wanted.

"I want to do what's right, God," he went on. "Please help me not to let you down tomorrow."

It took a few seconds, but there was no mistaking the peace that started to settle over Nick. He wanted to do right. God wanted him to do right. That made it pretty much unanimous. So what did he have to worry about?

A small smile crept over Nick's face as he rolled onto his side and pulled up the sheets. Sleep was on its way.

EIGHT
And the Winner Is . . .

It was my little buddy's big day. The school parking lot was packed with friends and followers of both our faithful fellow and his felonious foe. Being the great friend I am, I figured it could be a big day for me, too. Me, Howard the Hot-Dog Hawker.

"Get your programs, peanuts, popcorn, pickles, pinwheels, Pekinese . . ."

Pekinese!?

That's right. I'd tried all morning to get rid of the mutant mutt but no such luck. He just kept coming back. Why, I don't know. Either he liked the smell of the hot dogs or he thought I looked like a fire hydrant.

I'd snarled at him and he'd disappeared until . . . CHOMP. Well, there was no missing that feeling. The carnivorous canine had planted his pearly whites firmly into my sitting mechanism. I knew I needed to lose a few pounds, but this wasn't the weight-loss plan I had in mind. I tried to shake him off. Harder and harder and harder I shook. But he *wouldn't budge. (If this wasn't a case of "the tail wagging the dog," I don't know what would be!)*

Oh well, maybe if I bought a long coat and never sat down it wouldn't be so bad. Right, and chicken pox makes a great birthday present.

Then I spotted my good buddy Nick. I used to think he was a pretty good-sized kid. That is, until I saw him standing beside Derrick the Deadly in the parking lot. Suddenly I forgot all about my dog-gone (or dog-not-gone) problem. From the look of things, I knew I'd better get busy and sell the rest of my garbage, uh, souvenirs. You could never tell when your best buddy was going to need a little extra cash. I mean, hospital rooms run awfully high these days. . . .

It was nearly time to begin the race. A bunch of kids crowded around Louis as he drew a map of the race course with a piece of chalk. Nick and Derrick were there, decked out in their knee and elbow pads and helmets, peering over Louis's shoulder. It was clear to see he had outdone him-self. "Starting here," he said, "you both board up to Elm, then cut through the north end of the park. Complete the Trail of the Killer Worm, top to bottom, hit the rail, shoot the ramp, nail the cones, then haul down McKinley back here to the playground. First one across the finish line wins."

Translation: It was going to be one tough race.

"Let's get going," Louis said as he grabbed a flag and headed for the starting line. The rest of the kids followed.

Luckily Nicholas wasn't nervous. Not at all. Petrified, maybe. Terrified, yes. Near hysterical, with thoughts of *What have I done? What have I gotten into?* flashing though his mind . . . definitely. But nervous? Not a chance. He was too numb.

As Nick and Derrick set their skateboards on the line, Nick glanced at Derrick. The kid gave him his best Joker-vs.-Batman sneer. "You ready to die?" he growled.

To be honest, Nick hadn't given the idea much thought. After glancing at Derrick, though, it didn't seem that impossible. So much for his camping trip this summer.

"On your mark . . ." Louis raised the flag. The boys got on their boards. Maybe there was still some way out. Nicholas looked up to the sky— searching, hoping. Just one little tornado, that's all he needed. Or how about the ever-popular plague of locusts? He'd even settle for a good Russian missile streaking overhead. There was nothing.

"Get set . . ."

Nick turned to the crowd. Maybe he'd find help there. Once again, nothing. Except Philip. Poor kid. Everyone was still ignoring him and treating him like a goon. So he just stood off by himself, all alone . . . and very much afraid.

That's all it took. Suddenly Nicholas remembered very clearly what he had done, what he had gotten himself into . . . and why. None of this was for himself. It was for Philip. His fear started to disappear. OK, so maybe he wouldn't win. But he was going to bear down and give it his best shot . . . no matter what happened. One thing was for sure, Derrick was going to have to fight to win this one—because there was no way Nick was going to back down. Not now.

"GO!" Louis waved the flag. And they were off.

It was a good start. The kids clapped and cheered as the boys pushed off. Immediately Derrick took the lead. He was strong and fast. But Nick wasn't worried. It was going to be a long race. A lot could happen between now and the finish line. Besides, he wanted to save some energy for the end.

They started up the steep hill to the park. Nick's heart was pounding. Already he was breathing harder than he wanted. But Derrick just kept on pulling farther and farther away. So much for saving energy until the end. If Nick had any hope of winning he'd have to pull out all the stops and go full-speed now—and worry about the end later.

Nick bore down, skating harder and faster until he slowly started to close the gap. By the time they reached the top of the hill both boys were puffing hard. They looked down in front of them. There it was, "The Trail of the Killer Worm"—a twisting sidewalk that snaked dangerously down the steep hill.

They popped over the top and started down. They picked up speed so quickly that Derrick stopped skating and began to coast. Not Nick. His only hope of getting ahead of Derrick would be at places like this. So instead of coasting, he skated. Again and again he skated. Finally he was going so fast that the skating did no good. This was the fastest he had ever gone on a board—and it was terrifying. Most skaters would have tried to slow down. But Nick swallowed back his fear. He could not back off now. He had to win—for Philip. He forced himself to tuck down low, and picked up even more speed.

Finally Nick roared past Derrick. The big guy could only look on in amazement. This Martin kid had guts! Not to be outdone, Derrick followed suit. He tucked down and stayed right on Nick's tail. It was scary . . . for both of them. The sidewalk was a blur. Passersby were a streak of color (and an occasional startled shout). More than once Nick had to grab onto his board to keep his balance as he zoomed in and out of the treacherous curves. But he kept going.

Back at the finish line Renee looked around. Something was fishy . . . very fishy. She ran up to Louis who was talking to a couple of the guys.

"Louis," she said. "None of Derrick's clones are here."

He looked around. She was right. Not one of the Dorks was in sight. Louis frowned. Where were they? What were they up to?

"Come on," he said. "Let's check it out."
Together Nick's two friends dashed for their bikes.

Nick looked ahead and saw that the hill was starting to flatten out. He'd made it! The Trail of the Killer Worm was history! He pulled up from his tuck and began skating hard again. He pushed as quickly and powerfully as he could. So did

Derrick—and because Derrick was bigger and stronger, it wasn't long before he pulled away. Though Nick tried his best, he quickly lost ground.

Up ahead he could see the rail slide approaching. It was a bar set up six inches off the ground that ran ten feet down the middle of the sidewalk. Not a tough obstacle, but tough enough.

Derrick took it first. His form was excellent. He popped his board onto the bar, slid down to the end and popped it off. Perfect.

Nicholas followed. He dropped his weight to the back, kicked the board up onto the bar, and slid. It was a strange feeling, balancing on the bar, your wheels never touching. It only lasted a second, though. Then he had to pop his board back off. For a moment he almost lost it. The back wheel caught the bar and he started to fall. At the last second he caught himself, and somehow he managed to land squarely on the cement and keep moving.

Next came the launch ramp. Any smart skater knows you have to slow down for this. So Nick slowed down . . . a little. He hit the ramp, tucked down, grabbed his board, and shot off the top like a rocket. He was traveling so high and so fast it felt like he was in the air forever. He knew the landing would be hard. He was right. When he hit he felt it from his knees all the way into his chest. He'd worry about the pain later. Right now he had to build up speed and catch Derrick.

Not far away, in the park's restroom, the Dorks were at the sink. They were filling up a giant water balloon.

"What are you doing? Not so much!" Dork #1 ordered.

"Why not?" asked Dork #2. "Let's put this Martin kid out of business for good!" He turned the water on even harder.

Nick was starting to feel the cost of the race now. He felt it in his legs. They seemed to be turning into rubber; they were definitely starting to lose some feeling. He could also feel it in his lungs. They were beginning to burn, especially toward the back of his throat. But he kept pushing. Derrick was only a few feet ahead.

Before Nick knew it they were at the slalom—but instead of garbage cans, Louis had set up little red cones for them to weave through. No problem. At last, here was something Nicholas had practiced.

And the practice paid off.

The boys whisked past cone after cone. Slowly Nick closed in. Soon Derrick could hear his opponent's wheels. They were roaring just behind him. With every curve they sounded closer. Nick was practically on top of him. There was no need to look back. Derrick knew Nick was there. But he couldn't help himself. He had to check just to make sure. He only looked over his shoulder for a second—but a second was all it took.

When Derrick looked back to the course he saw the next cone coming—but it was coming too fast, too soon. He leaned hard and swerved. What luck! He missed it. But the turn was too tight. It threw him off-balance. Before he could catch himself he crashed into the next cone and went shooting off the sidewalk like a cannon.

Nicholas thundered past. His heart gave a leap. He was in the lead again! All right!

But would it last?

Derrick hopped on his board and began pursuit.

They hit another straight section. Derrick's strength and speed helped him catch up. Soon he was beside Nick. By the look of pain across their faces it was obvious that both boys were pushing to the limit. Derrick gave it everything he had and slowly pulled into the lead. Then somehow, some way, Nicholas found enough energy to bear down even more. Slowly he began to inch ahead. Not for long, though. Soon Derrick was beside him again. Then, ever so slowly he began to pull away—the inches gradually turned to feet, the feet into yards. Nick took his last ounce of strength and gave it his best and last effort . . .

It did no good. No matter what Nick tried, Derrick just kept inching further ahead.

Then, as if that weren't bad enough, Nicholas suddenly saw a huge yellow water balloon flying toward him. It exploded just feet in front of him. He tried to swerve and miss it but he was too close.

When his wheels hit the wet cement his board quickly slid out from under him. He crashed onto the concrete—hard—and began to tumble. Over and around and over again. He wondered if it would ever stop. There was no pain. That would come later. Right now there was nothing but tumbling and bouncing and rolling.

When Nick finally came to a stop he just lay

there, gasping for breath and staring at the sky. It was over. He had lost. A sick, sinking feeling spread through his stomach.

Then he heard it . . . laughter. He slowly raised his head and saw Derrick's Dorks. They were standing near one of the bushes having a good old time. Nick closed his eyes against the pounding in his head and the ache that filled his body. Well, at least he knew where the balloon had come from. "Let them have their laugh," he thought. "They've won . . . "

Then he heard another voice. Voices, actually: "Go get him, Nick! Do it, man! You can do it! Go!" He looked around. It was Louis and Renee. They had seen what had happened and were racing toward him, shouting for him to get up. But that's not what impressed Nicholas. I mean, they were his friends, they were supposed to encourage him. What impressed Nick was that they had the courage to do it right in front of the Dorks!

Nicholas struggled to sit up for a better look.

"Come on, Nick! You gotta beat him. Come on buddy!!"

Of course the Dorks shouted at Nick's friends and made the usual bone-crunching threats. But for the first time in their lives, his friends weren't backing down. It was like they were no longer afraid.

Nick could only wonder what had happened. It wouldn't be until later, when they all talked it over, that they'd really understand what had changed. Then they'd realize that what Nick had done out of love to help Philip had helped his friends as well. Somehow seeing Nick's stubborn love, a love that kept on loving regardless of the cost, had made them stronger. Somehow watching Nick had made them realize they didn't have to give in to kids like Derrick. I mean, hey, if Nick could do these things . . . well, they could, too.

Suddenly they were at Nick's side, helping him to his feet, grabbing his board. "Come on Nick, it's just a little further, you can still do it. Come on, man!"

He couldn't believe his ears. They'd been so afraid of standing up to Derrick. Now they were doing all they could to help Nick beat him.

The Dorks kept screaming and threatening, but it didn't seem to make any difference to Nick's friends. Not any more. His love had inspired them.

His love had given them strength.

They set the board on the sidewalk and helped him toward it. "Are you OK? You can do it. It's just a little farther."

Before he knew it Nick was standing beside his board. He turned to look at his two friends. He felt beat and broken. The last thing in the world he wanted to do was get back into the race. But how could he tell them that? Especially now, when they had finally taken his side? How could he let them down when they had finally found the courage to stand up to the bullies?

He couldn't. Without a word he took a deep breath, hoped on the board, and pushed off.

"All right! Way to go! Eat 'em up, Nick!"

Derrick seemed miles ahead. But Nick wouldn't give up. He couldn't. Not anymore. So he gave it everything he had. He skated and skated and then skated some more. His legs still felt numb. In fact, there were times he actually had to lift his skating leg up with his hands and force it back down again. But still he continued.

And, slowly, unbelievably, he began to close in on Derrick.

The Dorks saw what was happening. What was the kid doing? Didn't he know it was over? Why didn't he just give up? I mean, that's what he was supposed to do!

They began to panic. Nick was closing in fast. They had no alternative. They had to put Plan B into action.

Quickly they cut across the park to the spot where the course doubled back. From behind the bushes they pulled out three large garbage bags, stuffed full of leaves. As soon as Derrick zoomed past them they set the bags in the middle of the sidewalk. It was a perfect roadblock.

Nick rounded the corner and saw the bags right in front of him. What could he do? Another wipe-out would total him for good. He was nearly on top of them. Quickly, he threw his weight to the back of the board and kicked the nose up. Then he leaned forward and began to sail. He was doing an ollie! Just like he had practiced the day before. Only this was a perfect ollie, and it sent him sailing high over the bags.

When he came down he hit the concrete hard. He was a little shaky but managed to keep his balance and continue moving on. There was Derrick up ahead—just a few dozen yards from the finish line.

Nick skated and skated. The kids at the finish line started cheering him on. His chances were slim. But maybe, just maybe . . .

Wondering what all the cheering was about Derrick threw a look over his shoulder. He nearly wiped out in surprise. What was the kid doing so close? What did it take to put him away?

Nick continued to close in on Derrick. He was just a few feet ahead. But so was the finish line. Derrick spun around and began skating for all he was worth. For the first time anyone could remember Derrick Cryder actually looked worried.

Nick continued to skate. His lungs were on fire and he was starting to feel a little dizzy. He had never fainted before, but it didn't take a genius to figure out that that's what was about to happen.

Still he refused to give up. Derrick was less than two feet ahead. If only Nick could hold on.

Now Derrick was only a foot ahead.

Now six inches . . .

Then it happened . . .

Derrick crossed the finish line.

Derrick Cryder had won. It was close, but Derrick was the winner. The kids broke into cheers. Derrick came to a stop and raised his arms in victory, waiting for the crowd to surge around him and congratulate him.

It didn't happen. Instead, to Derrick's amazement, the crowd raced right past him. And ran to Nicholas.

"Great race, Nick!" they were shouting. "Awesome! Awesome all the way!" The kids crowded in on him from all sides. (Which was a good thing since he couldn't stand on his own anymore.) Louis grabbed his hand and lifted it high into the air. "The winner!" he shouted. "The winner!"

"What are you talking about?" Derrick yelled as he pushed his way into the crowd. "*I* won that race!!"

"Get lost, Derrick!" Suddenly a hush fell over the group. No one could believe their ears. Who would have the guts to talk to Derrick Cryder like that? They looked around. At first they didn't see anybody—but that's because they were looking too high.

"We won that race!" the courageous voice spoke up again. The kids' eyes widened in amazement

when they spotted who was talking. It was Philip! Little wimpy Philip!! He walked right up to Derrick, sticking his finger in the bully's chest. "We won because you cheated!" Philip said forcefully.

Derrick's mouth dropped open in amazement. All he could do was stare at the little pipsqueak. Philip didn't back down an inch. Like Louis and Renee, he, too, had been changed by Nicholas's love.

Suddenly another voice chimed in. "That's right!" It was Renee. "We saw you!"

Then the others joined in. At first everyone was shouting at once—then a chant started. "Derrick cheats, Derrick cheats, Derrick cheats. . . ."

Derrick tried to outshout them, to push at them, anything to regain control. But the crowd of kids would have none of it. "Derrick cheats, Derrick cheats, Derrick cheats . . ." Now everyone was standing up to Derrick Cryder. Finally, at long last, he had lost his power over them.

Lifting Nick on their shoulders they brushed past Derrick and headed off. Nick could only grin . . . and look down with amazement. Everyone . . . *everyone* had been changed. Philip, Louis, Renee, the crowd—even himself. All because he had obeyed God and shown a little love. Well, all right— maybe it wasn't so little. And it certainly wasn't as easy as he first thought.

But one thing was for sure: It worked!

NINE
Wrapping Up

Nick couldn't remember the walk home. In fact, he wasn't even sure he walked. For all he knew he could have floated. It sure felt like it. In any case, he reached the steps to his house and finally said good-bye to Philip.

"Thanks, Nicholas," the little guy said.

"Hey, no problem."

They shook hands, and Philip turned to head down the sidewalk. Nick watched for a moment. Was it just his imagination, or did the kid somehow seem a little taller? And his voice . . . had it gotten a little deeper? Finally Nick gave a shrug and started up the steps, only to run into Sarah.

"Oh, hi, Nick. Did you win your race?" Even Sarah seemed more friendly.

"Sorta . . . yeah. I guess I did."

"Great! I said a prayer for you."

Nicholas just stared. Was this really his sister talking? His arch rival? The one who had declared nonstop war against him for the rest of his life? "Really?" he managed to croak.

"Of course," she laughed. "You're my brother, aren't you?"

Nick just kept on staring.

She continued. "Listen, do me a favor. When Mom and Dad get home, tell them I went to the Robinsons to babysit."

"What happened to miniature golf?" he asked.

"Oh that . . ." She broke into a half smile. "Well, you know. It's not gonna hurt me to give a little once in a while. Right?"

"Right," Nick said, still not entirely believing his ears.

"Gotta run!" She bounced down the stairs past him. "Oh, and congratulations . . . Champ."

She gave him that smile again. I mean, it was almost like he was a human being. He smiled back. He couldn't help himself.

Boy, he thought. *This love stuff is really weird. Once it starts spreading, it's like there isn't any way of stopping it.* At least he hoped there wasn't.

"Champ, huh?" I stood on the sidewalk calling up to Nick. I was in my world-famous skater outfit: Foster Grant Goggles, Calvin Klein knee pads, Gucci helmet . . . and my ever-popular flowing white scarf. To be blunt, I looked awesome. To be frank, I was outrageous. To be honest, I was sweating like a pig. Maybe it was the scarf. Actually it wasn't my scarf. I had sneaked into little Jamie's room and "borrowed" it from her Barbie collection. But that's OK. I let Ken borrow my boxer shorts all the time. You know, the ones with the little green surfboards? Believe me, it makes the dude look,

like, you know, totally awesome, man.

"Stand back," I called to Nick as I reached down to my skateboard. It was just one of your standard, run-of-the-mill, rocket-powered skateboards. Kind of like Neil Armstrong used as the first skater to board on the moon. (We skaters have our own stories where history is concerned.) "Let a professional show you how it's really done," I shouted.

I gave the starting cord a yank. Nothing. I gave it another tug. Repeat performance. A third pull. Zippo. Finally I did what every professional skater learns in skateboard school. I punched its lights out.

The puppy roared to life. In fact, it roared into just a little too much life. There was so much smoke and fire that you could have barbecued a burger. Better make that a whole cow. Maybe a whole herd of whole cows.

Then off we zoomed. Well, actually not "we." The board zoomed just fine. I sort of got thrown into the air, did a half dozen flips, then crashed into the sidewalk—head first. Not a pretty sight. Except for the stars circling my brain. Made me wish I'd brought my telescope—I could see the big dipper there, Orion over there, and those . . . those were my shoes falling to the ground. (Fortunately my feet weren't in them.)

Slowly I realized my shoes weren't the only things I was missing. I felt inside my always grinning and perfectly shaped mouth. Empty. Rats. I hate it when that happens. Nothing ruins a good day like getting all your teeth knocked out.

"OK," Nicholas chuckled. "First you fall down

and hit your head. I got that. Now, what's my next lesson?"

"Ho-ho. Mery munny," I said as I got to my knees and began to search the sidewalk for my missing molars. "Now, melp me mind my meef."

Nick joined me in the search, but neither of us was too worried. Even if we didn't find them, Nicholas could just draw me another set. He'd have to. After all, our next adventure was going to be so scary, so spine-tingling, I'd have to have something to chatter.

So stay tuned, all you dudes and dudettes. . . .

Oh, and don't forget to floss. Remember, "healthy teeth are happy teeth!"